UNDER THE
GREAT PLUM TREE

Sufiya Ahmed ☀ Reza Dalvand

For Rehan, with all my love Api-Tiger
Sufiya Ahmed

For the golden hearts of Parisa and Elham
Reza Dalvand

For thousands of years, people have been telling stories.
From this rich global heritage, we can find stories that are
strikingly similar but also different. *One Story, Many Voices*
explores well-known stories from all over the world.

For teacher resources and more information,
visit www.tinyowl.co.uk
#GreatPlumTree

Copyright © Tiny Owl Publishing 2019
Text © Sufiya Ahmed 2019
Illustrations © Reza Dalvand 2019

Sufiya Ahmed has asserted her right under the Copyright, Designs
and Patents Act 1988 to be identified as Author of this work

Reza Dalvand has asserted his right under the Copyright, Designs
and Patents Act 1988 to be identified as Illustrator of this work

First published in the UK in 2019 and in the US in 2020 by Tiny Owl Publishing, London

A catalogue record for this book is available from the British Library.
A CIP record for this book is available from the Library of Congress.

ISBN 978-1-910328-46-0

Printed in China

UNDER THE
GREAT PLUM TREE

Sufiya Ahmed ☀ Reza Dalvand

TINY OWL

There once lived a monkey in India
with a **big golden heart**.

Her name was Miss Bandari.
All the animals in the jungle knew
she had a **heart of gold** and
that she was very **kind**.

One day, Miss Bandari was munching on a plum high up in her tree when she heard a groan down below on the riverbank.

She peeped through the branches to see the old crocodile Mr. Magarmach crawl up to seek the shade of the tree.

"Hello,"
called Miss Bandari.

"How are you today?"

Mr. Magarmach sighed.

"A bit tired and hungry,
actually. I'm too old to hunt now."

Miss Bandari's big golden heart felt sad.

"Would you like a plum?"
she asked, trying to cheer him up.

"It's very sweet."

Mr. Magarmach snapped open
his jaws and caught the fruit
between his old, rotted teeth.

From that day on Mr. Magarmach visited Miss Bandari every day.
They became very good friends as they munched plums together.

Mr. Magarmach
told exciting stories
about a time when he had
been strong, brave, and bold.

There were tales of human hunters, pythons, and lions. Miss Bandari clapped her hands and listened in wonder at the adventures of the past.

One afternoon Mr. Magarmach
crawled up to the great plum tree.
Miss Bandari looked down.

**"What stories have you got
for me today?"** she cried.

"No tales today, Miss Bandari,"
said Mr. Magarmach.

"Instead, I would like to repay your kindness.
Would you like to come for lunch?"

"Yes please!" she exclaimed.

So Miss Bandari jumped onto Mr. Magarmach's
scaly green back and off they went.

On their way, they saw Dame Hati
by the riverbank. She was so surprised to see
them that water snorted out of her trunk!

"Where are you off to?" she called.

"I'm going to Mr. Magarmach's for lunch,"
Miss Bandari said proudly.

"But King Crocodile lives in the swamp
along the river," cried Dame Hati.
"You can't go there. **He will eat you!**"

Miss Bandari's big golden heart
thumped loudly in her chest.
She was very frightened.

"Is this true?
Are you taking me to
King Crocodile for his lunch?"

Mr. Magarmach stopped swimming.
"Don't be silly, Miss Bandari. King Crocodile
has heard of your big golden heart
and he only wants to see it."

"Well, well,"
said Dame Hati,
looking very wise.

"There's no point
taking Miss Bandari
there empty-handed.
Even my old eyes can see
she's left her golden heart
back in her tree."

Miss Bandari looked down
at her empty hands.

Then at Dame Hati.

Dame Hati winked
and her eye twinkled...

"Yes. Yes!" cried Miss Bandari,
jumping up and down on
Mr. Magarmach's scaly green back.

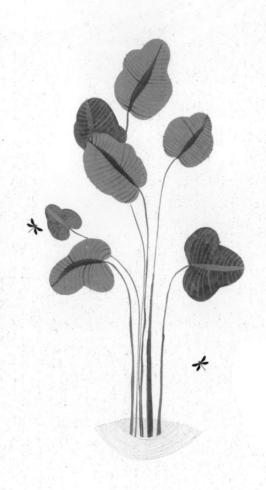

"My heart is in my tree. Please take me back
so I can collect it. King Crocodile will not be
pleased to see us arrive without it," she said.

"You're very silly," grumbled Mr. Magarmach
as he swam back.

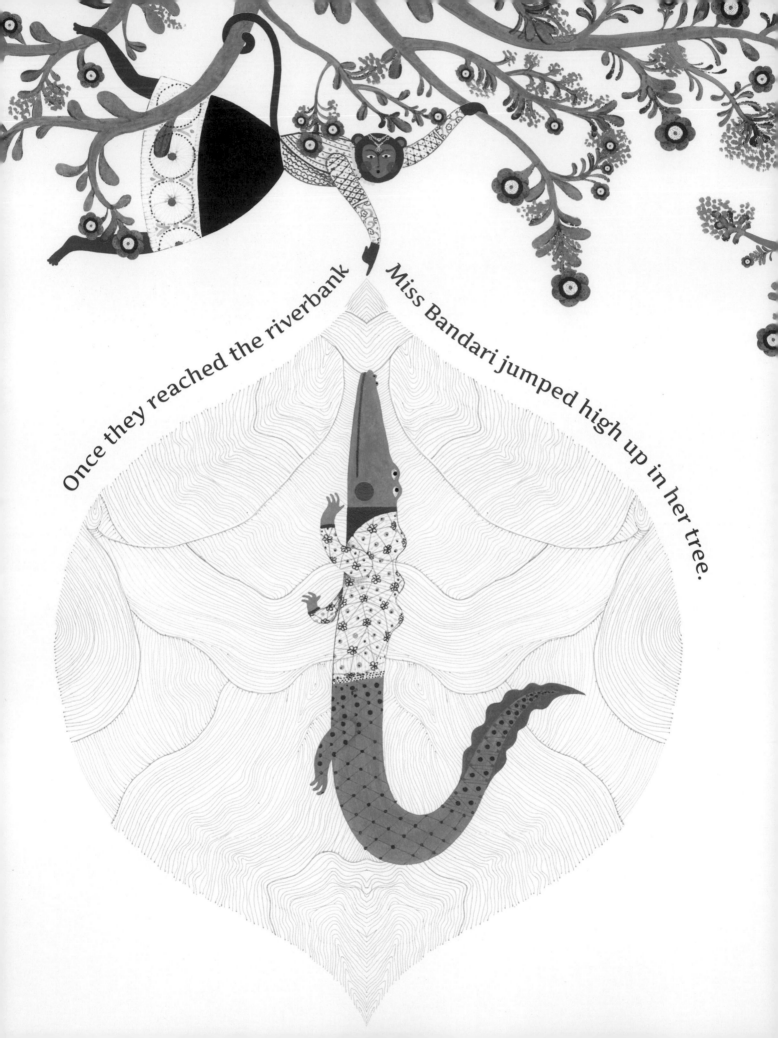

Once they reached the riverbank Miss Bandari jumped high up in her tree.

"Mr. Magarmach, you're the one
who is silly. My heart was always inside me
and not in my tree. Dame Hati tricked you.
She is my true friend, unlike you."

Big tears rolled down Mr. Magarmach's face
as he swam away. He had lost his best friend.

Back in the swamp, King Crocodile's giant tail
swished angrily. He looked mean and hungry.

"Where is my big golden heart
that tastes like plum tart?" he snapped.

Mr. Magarmach's own heart sank.
Dame Hati and Miss Bandari had been right.
King Crocodile was going to eat his friend!

King Crocodile bared his sharp teeth. "I told you to bring Miss Bandari to me!"

Suddenly Mr. Magarmach felt very brave. "No," he said, standing tall. "I will not bring you Miss Bandari's big golden heart. She is my friend."

King Crocodile looked like he would explode with anger.
"Then you cannot live in my swamp," he snarled.

"Very well," said Mr. Magarmach,
slowly swimming away.
"I would rather live alone than hand
my friend over to you."

A few days
later Miss Bandari
was swinging between
the trees when she saw
Mr. Magarmach lying in the
river. He looked old and cold.

Miss Bandari's big golden
heart felt sad.

"Mr. Magarmach," she called.
"You can live under my tree. It will give you
shade and I will share my plums. But you
must promise that you will never be fooled
by King Crocodile again."

Mr. Magarmach smiled.
"I promise!"

And so Mr. Magarmach found a new home
on the riverbed where he happily ate the
plums from Miss Bandari's tree.

Mr. Magarmach still told stories from
the past but it was his bravery against
King Crocodile that he loved
to tell the most.

Sufiya Ahmed wrote this book about a kind-hearted monkey and a silly old crocodile after listening to her mother's tales about the Indian jungle. In Hindi, Bandari means monkey and Magarmach means crocodile!

Reza Dalvand's illustrations are inspired by Indo-Persian traditions. He loves using bright patterns and designs from various cultures, so that his books talk to people from around the world.